The William Shakespeare

CHILDREN'S COLLECTION

Dados Internacionais de Catalogação na Publicação (CIP) de acordo com ISBD

S527a Shakespeare, William
As you like it / William Shakespeare. - Jandira, SP : W. Books, 2025.
96 p. ; 12,80cm x 19,80cm. - (Classics).

ISBN: 978-65-5294-205-0

1. Literatura inglesa. 2. Clássicos. 3. Aventura. 4. Fantasia. 5. Imaginação. I. Título.
II. Série.

2025-2508 CDD 823
CDU 821.111

Elaborada por Lucio Feitosa - CRB-8/8803
Índice para catálogo sistemático:
1. Literatura inglesa : 823
2. Literatura inglesa : 821.111-31

Text based on the original play by William Shakespeare,
adapted by Gemma Barder
Cover Illustrations by Rishabh Goswami
Internal Illustrations by Adrián Jiménez

1st edition in 2025
www.cirandacultural.com.br

EASY CLASSICS
William Shakespeare
As You Like It
W. Books

Rosalind
Daughter of
Duke Senior

Celia
Daughter of Duke
Frederick

Duke Senior
Rosalind's father and
Duke Frederick's brother

Duke Frederick
Celia's father and
Duke Senior's brother

Orlando & Oliver

Sons of Sir Rowland de Boys

Corin, Silvius & Phoebe

Shepherds and shepherdess

Chapter One

Pacing angrily around the royal court, Orlando couldn't hold in his frustration. His father, Sir Rowland de Boys, had recently died, leaving Orlando and his two brothers Oliver and Jacques. Oliver, the eldest, had inherited everything and was now the head of the family.

Oliver hated Orlando who was handsome, well-liked and much stronger than him. Oliver couldn't stand it, so he decided that he wouldn't give his brother any money.

Orlando was furious. 'Father told you to give me a good education, like Jacques, but instead you treat me like a servant,' he shouted at his brother. 'How can I make something of myself with no money and no opportunities?'

Oliver didn't care. He folded his arms and refused to listen to his brother.

'I know Father set some money aside for me,' said Orlando. 'Give it to me.'

'You know what?' sneered Oliver. 'You can have that money and go. And take old Adam with you. He's a worthless servant but seems to like you for some reason.'

'Worthless?' Adam gasped. 'Sir Rowland would never have spoken to me like that!'

Adam and Orlando left to gather their things, and Oliver

stared after them, smiling nastily. He had no intention of giving his brother any money at all.

Moments later, a visitor arrived to see Oliver. It was Charles, Duke Frederick's wrestler.

'My lord,' Charles said. 'I am wrestling at the new duke's palace tomorrow to celebrate him taking power. I have learnt that your younger brother, Orlando, plans to come and wrestle me. As you know, I'm the best wrestler there is, so obviously

I will beat him. Perhaps you can talk him out of humiliating himself?'

As Oliver listened, an idea began to form. Perhaps there was a way to get rid of his brother for ever. 'I am afraid I already know that Orlando plans to fight,' he lied. 'And unfortunately, there's

no reasoning with my brother. But you should know that he is a true villain. If you were to beat him, he wouldn't rest until he got his revenge. You'd never be safe as long as he is alive. If I were you, I'd make sure he doesn't survive the fight.'

Charles was horrified. 'Thank you for your advice, my lord. I will make sure that he doesn't walk away from our wrestling match.'

As Charles left, Oliver smiled to himself. Soon the brother that he hated, but whom everyone else loved, would be gone forever.

Meanwhile, another drama was unfolding on the estate next to

Oliver's. The kindly old Duke Senior had been overpowered by his younger brother, Frederick, and banished into the nearby Forest of Arden.

One person who hadn't been banished was Duke Senior's daughter, Rosalind. Frederick hadn't sent her away because she was his niece and best friends with his daughter, Celia. Rosalind had agreed to stay, even though it broke her heart to see her father leave.

Celia was good to Rosalind and bitterly ashamed of what her father had done. 'As soon as I inherit everything from him, I will give it all back to you,' she promised Rosalind.

'I refuse to have a stolen title or a stolen home.'

'You are a good friend,' Rosalind said, hugging Celia. She didn't know what she would do without her cousin's kindness.

That particular day, Rosalind was missing her father badly. 'Come for a walk,' Celia said. 'It will do you good.'

'I'll come, but it won't bring my father back,' Rosalind replied sadly.

Chapter Two

As they walked, an elderly servant came to tell the girls that the wrestling contest had started. 'It's very exciting,' he said. 'Charles, the duke's wrestler, is winning so far. Three brothers challenged him. And one by one, Charles broke their ribs and defeated them.'

'I'm not sure I want to watch that,' said Rosalind.

Just then, there was a fanfare as Celia's father, Duke Frederick, approached. He was surrounded by lords, servants, Charles and a young man, who was half the wrestler's size.

'As you're so determined to fight, I won't stop you,' the duke laughed, clapping the young man on the back.

'That man can't possibly fight Charles,' Rosalind cried. 'He will be killed.'

Rosalind and Celia hurried over to the young man, who was in fact, Orlando.

'Please don't fight,' pleaded Rosalind. 'Nobody will think any less of you.'

Orlando smiled. 'If I win, then all will be well. If I lose, I have no friends to miss me.'

The girls could see there was no point in trying to talk Orlando out of the fight. They stepped back and sadly wished him luck.

The fight started and to everyone's surprise, it was an even match. The crowd watched nervously as both Orlando and Charles tried to gain the advantage.

Again and again, they grappled and released, neither man able to find the winning move. Until suddenly, one of them was thrown to the ground. The crowd stood aghast, mouths open, as Charles lay motionless on the floor. Duke Frederick walked over to congratulate Orlando. 'What is your name, young man?' he asked.

'Orlando, youngest son of Sir Rowland de Boys!' he replied proudly. The duke's expression darkened.

grapple

To wrestle with an opponent by clutching or gripping.

'That is a shame. Your father was my enemy,' he said bluntly. He walked away without giving Orlando the prize money for the fight. Celia rolled her eyes, embarrassed by her father's behaviour.

Rosalind felt sorry for Orlando. She took off her necklace and gave it to him. 'Please take this and wear it for me. My father loved Sir Rowland, as did the rest of the world,' she said.

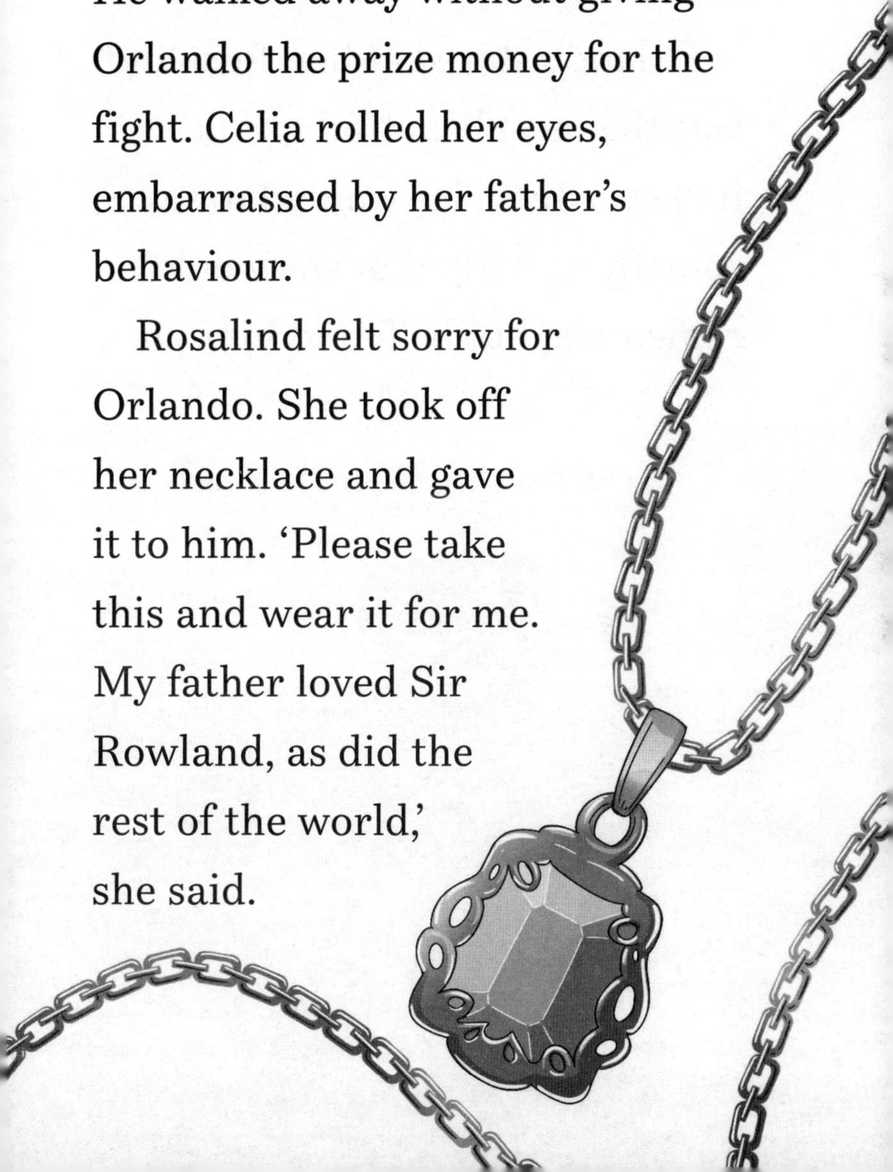

'I would give you more, but I have nothing since my father was sent away.'

Orlando stared at her. Rosalind was the most beautiful girl he had ever seen. He wanted to say something witty that she would remember, but he found himself

struggling for words. After an awkward silence, Celia took Rosalind's hand. 'Congratulations. A well-deserved victory,' she said to Orlando, before turning and quickly walking away, pulling Rosalind along behind her.

Orlando put a hand over his face. *Why couldn't I just speak to her?* he thought. 'Excuse me,' he said to one of the courtiers. 'Who is that girl?' He pointed, as Rosalind turned to look back one last time before disappearing with Celia.

'That is Rosalind, daughter of the banished Duke Senior,' the courtier replied.

'Rosalind,' Orlando mused as he examined the necklace she had given him.

Chapter Three

Rosalind couldn't stop thinking about the young man. She had

never believed in love at first sight until now. Celia smiled as she watched Rosalind skipping about humming to herself. 'You like him!' she teased, laughing.

Before Rosalind could answer, Duke Frederick burst in, eyes filled with anger.

'Go! Leave my court now,' he shouted at Rosalind. 'If I find you within twenty miles of here in ten days' time, you'll pay with your life!'

Rosalind was taken aback. 'Me? What have I done, Uncle?'

'I don't trust you,' he spat. 'You are your father's daughter and that's enough for me!'

'I've done nothing wrong,' Rosalind said, stubbornly.

Celia couldn't take any more. 'She's not a traitor and nor was her father! She's here for me. If you banish her, you banish me.'

Duke Frederick glared at his daughter. 'She is cunning. Her being here makes you look bad. She is banished and I'll hear no more about it.' He stormed out.

Celia hugged Rosalind. 'I won't let you go alone. I'm coming with you, no matter what you say. We'll run away and live with your father in the Forest of Arden,' she said.

‘It’s too dangerous for two girls to travel alone,’ Rosalind replied, moved by her cousin’s love.

‘We could dress in ripped clothes with dirt on our faces. We’ll make new identities. I’ll call myself Aliena!’ said Celia.

Rosalind thought for a moment. ‘Well, seeing as I’m so tall, I could dress as a man. I’ll be Ganymede,’ she added.

They decided to leave straight away. That afternoon, they crept out of the house and slipped

identity

The set of characteristics by which a person or thing is recognised or known.

through the gardens. Nobody spotted them as they hurried away.

In the depths of the Forest of Arden, Duke Senior was finding life away from the royal court quite pleasing. Several of the lords of the land who had served the duke had refused to accept Duke Frederick and had followed him into the forest. Although they didn't have very much, they soon learnt how to live among the trees.

'It's a simple and good life,' the old duke told them. 'We are away from danger and the noise of the city. We hear the wind in the trees, read books and live a free life,' he said, taking in a deep breath. The lords all agreed they would not want to be anywhere else.

Back at court, Duke Frederick was furious that his daughter and niece had disappeared without anyone noticing. He had the whole house and the grounds searched, but there was no sign of the girls anywhere.

'Did no one see them go?' he shouted, staring at his lords with bulging eyes. They all shook their heads in response.

'My lord. The maid overheard Celia and Rosalind giggling about the wrestler boy – maybe they have gone somewhere with him?' one lord suggested.

The duke looked even more annoyed. 'Someone go and speak to Oliver de Boys right now. Tell him I want his brother found and brought to me immediately!'

As one of his servants bowed and turned to leave, the duke held up his hand. 'If Oliver can't find his brother, then bring Oliver himself. Someone will answer for this family's behaviour.'

Adam rushed to meet Orlando when he arrived home. 'Sir.

You can't go inside,' he warned, blocking Orlando's path.

Orlando looked confused. 'Why not? What's happened?'

Adam started to explain. He was trembling and spoke quickly. 'It's your brother. When he heard that you beat the duke's wrestler, he lost his temper. He wanted you to die in the fight. Now that plan has failed, he's planning to burn your house down while you sleep tonight. He will see you dead one way or another. You must leave.'

The news wasn't a huge surprise

to Orlando. He'd lived with his brother's hate for as long as he could remember. 'But where would I go?' he asked. 'I have no money to start a new life.'

'I have some money saved. I will go with you, we'll find a way,' Adam said, desperately.

Orlando looked at Adam, who had served his father so faithfully. Orlando admired his loyalty and knew he had received more love and kindness from this man than he ever had from his own brother.

He agreed to leave with him, promising himself that he'd repay the kindness Adam had shown him. Together the two of them left to find a new life elsewhere.

Chapter Four

Celia and Rosalind had reached the Forest of Arden and were worn out. They were tired and hungry. 'I can't go on much longer,' Celia declared, worried about how they would find their next meal.

Through the trees they spotted two shepherds talking together.

'Nobody has ever felt the way I feel about Phoebe,' said the younger shepherd.

'Of course, Silvius. No one else in the world has ever been in love,' laughed the older shepherd.

‘It sounds like Silvius feels the same way I do,’ Rosalind whispered to Celia.

‘I don’t care about that right now! Ask them if we can buy some food,’ she sighed, clutching her growling stomach.

Remembering she was now pretending to be Ganymede, Rosalind walked over, trying to appear casual. ‘Do you know of a place we can rest and buy food?’ she asked. ‘My friend is tired and hungry.’

The shepherd turned around in surprise. ‘Hello, fair sir. I work for a master who is not very generous, so I have little to give you. But this cottage is empty, and you are welcome to stay in it.'

The cousins looked at each other. 'Yes, please,' cried Celia.

The shepherd grinned back at them. 'Of course! Come with me. I'll show you around and you can rest,' he replied.

Not far from the Forest of Arden, Adam was also tired and hungry. Orlando noticed and told him to sit. 'You're okay. You just need food. Wait here and I'll bring you some,' he told Adam reassuringly. Adam sank down by a tree to rest, while Orlando headed into the woods in search of food.

Orlando pushed on through the trees. Before long he heard the sound of men laughing and chatting. He crept closer and as he peered through the trees, he saw them. They sat at a table that had a small amount of food laid out.

Taking a deep breath, he approached. 'Nobody touch anything else until I've got what I want!' he shouted, trying to sound as dangerous as he could.

Orlando didn't realise he was talking to the old duke and the banished lords.

Duke Senior jumped up. 'Are you distressed, or simply lacking good manners?' he asked, as his lords stared at Orlando in bewilderment.

'I'm almost starving. I have manners. I was raised with a proper upbringing, but I must have food,' Orlando begged.

'Of course, but put your sword away,' said the duke. Gesturing towards the table he spoke to Orlando with warmth. 'Come and sit at the table, have food. We see

bewilderment

A feeling of being confused or disoriented.

you are a gentleman. We've also seen better days, but today this is what we have.'

Orlando felt ashamed of his behaviour. 'You are very kind. I was trying to be fierce because I thought the forest was a savage place. I'm truly sorry.' He put his sword away. 'I'd love to join you, but first, I must get my friend, Adam. He's walked with me for many miles, but he is tired and weak,' he explained. The group promised that both were welcome and that they wouldn't touch a bite of food until they returned.

Orlando returned, holding Adam in his arms. The lords rushed to help, placing food and drink in front of them, so everyone could eat together. Through mouthfuls of food, Orlando explained how he and Adam had come to be in the forest.

'I see the resemblance now,' Duke Senior smiled at Orlando. 'I loved Sir Rowland, your father, and you are truly welcome here,' he exclaimed.

Chapter Five

Meanwhile, Oliver was brought before Duke Frederick.

'Where is your brother?' the duke demanded.

'I don't know!' cried Oliver.

'I don't believe you,' the duke sneered. 'Unless you bring him to me within the next few days, I will take everything you own. Your money, your home – everything.'

'I'm not protecting him! I hate my brother. If I knew where he was, I would tell you immediately!'

The duke glared at him. 'So, you are both useless *and* have no decency,' he said coldly. 'Get out of my sight and find your brother.'

'Yes, my lord,' muttered Oliver, barely concealing his anger.

'Take his possessions and throw him out,' the duke told his men. 'I have no more use for him.'

Corin the shepherd was resting under a tree, when Rosalind, still dressed as a boy, wandered past. She was reading aloud from a piece of paper: 'Let no face be kept in mind. But the fair of Rosalind.' The shepherd began to laugh.

'That's the worst poem I've ever heard,' he said. 'It doesn't even rhyme. Did you write it yourself?'

'I found it pinned on a tree,' Rosalind said.

The shepherd shook his head and wandered back to work.

Celia disguised as Aliena appeared, giggling as she read a similar note out loud: 'I write words to hang from trees, to be carried by the wind, with sentences made to please, all ending with Rosalind.' She looked at her cousin with a grin. 'These poems are everywhere, and they're all about you.'

'But who wrote them?' Rosalind asked.

'Can't you guess?' Celia teased.

'No! Tell me who!' Rosalind demanded, growing impatient.

'Orlando!' Celia giggled.

Embarrassed, Rosalind blushed. 'How do you know?' she asked.

'I saw him under a tree, dressed like a hunter,' Celia laughed. Before she could say anything more, Orlando came walking towards them.

Rosalind jumped to her feet and hid behind the cattle shed. She gestured for Celia to follow and placed a finger to her lips.

‘Why did this have to happen when I’m living as a boy? I can’t risk breaking my disguise.’

The pair watched as Orlando got closer. Rosalind couldn’t bear to be so near without being able to speak to him.

‘I’m going to talk to him,’ she decided. ‘Even if he doesn’t know who I am.’ She stepped out from behind the shed and put on her best male voice. ‘Who are you?’ she called.

Orlando spun around, surprised.

‘Nobody,’ he replied. ‘Do you live here?’

‘Yes, I live with my sister here, on the outskirts of the forest. Been here all my life,’ she answered. She could see Orlando was surprised.

‘Your accent sounds far too fine to have grown up here,’ he said.

‘Well, it isn’t,’ Rosalind said. ‘Are you the one who’s been leaving the notes on all the trees?’

Orlando’s eyes widened. ‘Yes,’ he said. ‘It’s because I can never be with the girl I love.’

Rosalind hid her pleasure at hearing this news. She was

determined to keep seeing Orlando, even if he could never know who she was. Thinking quickly, she said: ‘I can cure you of it, if you want. You can visit me every day and pretend I’m Rosalind. I’ll be so horrible to you that you’ll soon fall out of love.’

Orlando shook his head. ‘I don’t think anyone could cure me.’

‘I bet I can,’ said Rosalind. ‘Come back this time tomorrow and we’ll start.’

Chapter Six

The next day, Rosalind waited and waited for her secret love to appear, but Orlando didn't appear. 'Where is he, Celia? He said he'd come!' she cried.

They were interrupted as Corin burst in through the door.

'You have to come right now. Silvius is declaring his love to Phoebe, and you won't want to miss it.'

Celia jumped up and grabbed Rosalind's hand. 'Come on, Ganymede. Maybe we can help.'

They hurried into the forest where Silvius was on his knees in front of a young woman. 'I can't live without your love,' the young shepherd begged.

‘I don’t love you, Silvius,’ the young woman said, turning her face away. ‘Please just leave me alone.’

Rosalind felt sorry for the shepherd. ‘Why do you treat this

poor man like this?’ she asked Phoebe crossly. ‘Were you not brought up correctly? You should be thankful for the love of a good man. And you,’ she said looking at Silvius, ‘Why follow her around, you foolish shepherd? You’re better than this!’

Phoebe's mouth fell open. She had never heard anyone speak to her like that in her whole life. She decided she quite liked it. Also, the stranger was very attractive. Phoebe decided she had fallen head over heels in love with this 'Ganymede'.

'Let's go,' Rosalind said to Celia. 'Keep working on her,' she whispered to Silvius.

'Don't be so proud,' she shouted to Phoebe, who was still gazing at her in admiration.

As Rosalind and Celia wandered back, they found Orlando waiting at the cottage.

'Where have you been?' Rosalind said, pretending to be Ganymede, pretending to be Rosalind, as she had promised.

Orlando played along. 'My beautiful Rosalind. I come within an hour of the time we agreed.'

'Every second counts when you're in love,' Rosalind scolded him. 'If you really loved me, you wouldn't be able to be away from me for a moment.'

At this point Celia couldn't resist joining in, 'You do know he has another Rosalind somewhere with a prettier face!' she smiled, holding in a laugh as Rosalind shot her a look.

'I hope Rosalind won't frown at me like you do. It would kill me!' said Orlando sadly.

Rosalind softened. 'Ask me what you want, and I will give it,' she suggested.

'I want you to love me, Rosalind!' Orlando asked.

'Okay, I will on Fridays and Saturdays,' she replied, almost forgetting she was acting as Ganymede.

'But what about the other days?' he asked.

'You can never have too much of a good thing,' Rosalind teased him.

Orlando looked into her eyes and for a moment Rosalind thought her cover would be blown. 'I'm afraid, I have to go,' he said. 'I must attend the duke's lunch. I'll come back later.'

Rosalind turned and folded her arms, pretending to be cross. 'You have only just declared your love and now you're casting me aside,' she said. 'You had better be back later, or our love is over.'

Orlando laughed and promised to be back. As he left, Rosalind let out a huge sigh. 'I can't bear to be away from him,' she sighed. 'I don't know what to do with myself until he comes back.'

Chapter Seven

A few hours later, Rosalind was still waiting for Orlando to return, when Silvius came running over, clutching a letter. 'Phoebe asked me to give this to you, sir,' he panted, handing it over to Rosalind.

Rosalind opened the letter and began to read, scrunching her face as she did. 'Phoebe says she will never love Silvius, and that she loves me instead,' she said, her face scrunching even further. 'And if I

don't return her love she will die.'
She turned to look at Silvius. 'Why on earth do you like this woman?' she asked.

Silvius shrugged. 'I can't help it,' he said. 'I love her.'

Rosalind looked at him, her eyes softening in sympathy. 'Okay,' she said. 'Go to her and tell her that if she truly loves me, she can prove it by doing what I say and loving you. If she will not do that, then I will never love her, unless you ask me to.'

The shepherd looked confused.

'Go on,' smiled Rosalind. 'It will work I promise.'

Celia watched him go. 'Poor shepherd,' she sighed. As she turned to speak to Rosalind, she noticed a man hurrying towards them.

‘Good morning. Could you tell me where the shepherd’s cottage is? It belongs to a boy and his sister,’ he asked.

Celia blushed a little. ‘That’s us,’ she said.

Oliver held out a handkerchief covered in blood. ‘Orlando asked me to give this to you,’ he explained.

The girls stared at the handkerchief in shock.

‘What’s happened?’ gasped Rosalind. ‘Is Orlando okay?’

‘Orlando was on his way here,’ the stranger began, ‘when he came across a man asleep under a tree.

He saw that a snake had wrapped itself around the man's neck. Orlando jumped into action and scared the snake away. But then, Orlando saw a lioness with her cubs crouched in the trees, getting ready to pounce on the sleeping man. Orlando looked at the man again and realised that it was his older brother.'

'Oh, I've heard him talk of this brother,' Celia interrupted. 'He sounds horrible.'

The stranger nodded, agreeing, 'Yes. He's not a nice man. But Orlando is much kinder than his brother, and he couldn't stand by and watch the lioness attack him. He fought the lioness and eventually defeated her. That's when I woke up.' The stranger stared at the ground.

‘You are the brother?’ Rosalind asked.

‘The one who tried to kill him?’ Celia added.

Oliver nodded, embarrassed. ‘I am ashamed of who I was. I have changed, I swear. Orlando and I talked, and he took me to see the duke. It was only when Orlando went to change his clothes that he realised he had been injured by the lioness. His arm is bleeding, and the duke is looking after him. He sent me to show you this and tell you that he would have been here if he could.’

Oliver held up the handkerchief. Rosalind was so worried at the sight of Orlando's blood that she fainted.

'Ganymede!' Celia cried, rushing forwards to catch her.

'Ha-ha!' Rosalind laughed awkwardly as she came round. She thought quickly, worried that she had blown her cover. 'Um, I didn't really faint. I was acting the part of Orlando's lover. Please tell him just how well I played the part.'

'Oh yes, well done,' said Celia, rolling her eyes at her cousin.

'Please tell Orlando we'll see him as soon as he is well enough,' said Rosalind.

'Come back to our cottage and rest for a while before your journey back,' Celia suggested to Oliver, blushing prettily.

'You are too kind,' Oliver said. 'I'd love to.'

Rosalind watched as the pair walked ahead of her, giggling with each other as they went. It seemed as though love was in the air.

Chapter Eight

Orlando stared at his brother in shock. 'You're in love with Aliena?' he asked, shocked.

Oliver moved closer, his eyes dancing. 'All I want is to marry her and for us to live in a cottage together and be shepherds. I don't need anything else.'

Taking Oliver's hand, Orlando smiled. 'Brother, you

have my approval. Go and ask her. You can be married tomorrow if she says yes.'

As Oliver hurried away, Rosalind – still dressed as Ganymede – arrived to see Orlando.

'I'm sorry to see you in pain,' she said. 'Did Oliver tell you how well I acted, pretending to faint?'

'Yes, and so much more,' he laughed.

Rosalind grinned. 'Don't tell me! Oliver and Aliena. They've fallen head over heels for each other.'

'They'll be married tomorrow,' Orlando said. He looked at Rosalind and let out a heavy sigh. 'It will be hard to see them so happy when I can't have the one I want.'

Rosalind's heart ached. She knew she couldn't keep up this act. She didn't want to.

'I can help you,' she said quickly. 'If you love Rosalind as much as you say, I can make her appear in front of your eyes tomorrow.'

He looked at her questioningly. 'Honestly?'

Rosalind nodded, smiling. 'Yes. Put on your finest clothes, invite your friends. You'll marry Rosalind tomorrow!'

Orlando stared at her in wonder, but before he could reply, Silvius

and Phoebe appeared. Phoebe looked very angry. 'You shouldn't have shared that letter with others!' she told Rosalind. 'It was private!'

Rosalind shrugged her shoulders. 'You should love Silvius instead!'

Phoebe turned to Silvius, 'Tell Ganymede what it means to be in love,' she said.

‘It means to be faithful, devoted, patient and suffer as I do for Phoebe,’ he declared.

‘And I for Ganymede,’ Phoebe added.

‘And I for Rosalind,’ Orlando added.

Rosalind took a deep breath. ‘I’ll help you all,’ she said, smiling. ‘Come here tomorrow. Phoebe, you have my word, if I ever marry a woman, it will be you. And tomorrow I am getting married!’

Phoebe smiled in delight.

Rosalind looked at Orlando. ‘And I promise, you will also be married tomorrow. As will you, Silvius. Trust me. Your happiness counts on it.'

The next morning, Duke Senior arrived in the clearing with Orlando and Oliver. Phoebe and Silvius were already waiting, as was Celia – still dressed as Aliena.

'Do you really think Ganymede will bring Rosalind?' the duke asked Orlando.

'I can only hope,' answered Orlando.

Rosalind, dressed as Ganymede, hurried into the clearing. 'If I bring your daughter, will you let Orlando marry her?' she asked her father. The duke nodded, not realising his own daughter was right in front of him. 'Of course, if that's what she wanted,' he replied.

Rosalind turned to Orlando. 'And you will definitely marry Rosalind if she comes here?' she asked.

'Without hesitation,' he answered.

Finally, Rosalind looked at Phoebe, 'And if for any reason you refuse to marry me, will you marry Silvius instead?' she asked.

Phoebe nodded. 'But there is nothing you can do to make me not want to marry you.'

Rosalind smiled and turned to Silvius. 'And you'll marry Phoebe if she's willing?'

'Yes, of course,' he nodded.

'Then you must all remember what you have promised,' Rosalind said. 'I must leave for a moment. When I return everything will be clear,' she said and hurried away, pulling Celia behind her.

Moments later, everyone watched in disbelief as Rosalind and Celia strolled back into the forest. The duke had tears in his eyes as he said, 'Rosalind! You're here!'

Rosalind turned to Phoebe and held up the hat she had been wearing as Ganymede.

Phoebe gasped. 'You were him?' She looked devastated.

Rosalind reached for her hand. 'I'll never marry another woman, I promise,' she laughed.

'Well, I gave my word, and I won't break it.' Phoebe moved closer towards Silvius. 'I will try to

make you happy,' she said. Silvius threw his arms around her.

Oliver took Celia's hand in his. 'I don't care if you're a woman of wealth or a shepherdess, I would marry you a thousand times.'

Orlando looked overwhelmed, as he stared at Rosalind. 'It's you.'

‘I’m yours if you want me,’ she whispered back.

The duke cleared his throat and stepped forward. ‘You all wish to be married?’ he asked.

‘We do!’ they answered as one.

And so, the duke married them all immediately.

As the wedding celebrations began a man burst into the clearing. 'It's our brother!' cried Oliver to Orlando.

It was indeed Jacques de Boys. 'I bring news,' he said. 'Duke Fredrick gathered an army to come here and overpower you.'

Everyone looked anxious and Phoebe let out a gasp.

'However, on his way, he met a religious man who converted him,' Jacques added quickly. 'Frederick has changed his ways. He has decided to become a holy man and live a simple life. He has returned all your titles and lands.'

The duke grinned, stunned at how this evening was turning out. 'There couldn't be a better wedding gift,' he said. 'We will return, but first, we still have celebrating to do. This calls for

dancing,' he declared brightly.

As the party continued through the night, Rosalind moved away to the clearing's edge and looked up at the moon. *What a long and peculiar journey it has been*, she

thought. Then, as she watched her friends and family, she spoke softly to herself, 'But I certainly like how it has ended!' Grinning happily, she walked back to rejoin the celebrations.